WITH SPECIAL THANKS TO LINDA CHAPMAN

First published in Great Britain in 2012 by Simon and Schuster UK Ltd
A CBS COMPANY

Text Copyright © Hothouse Fiction Limited 2012
Illustrations copyright © Mary Hall 2012
Designed by Amy Cooper

3 5 7 9 10 8 6 4 2

Simon & Schuster UK Ltd
1st Floor, 222 Gray's Inn Road
London
WC1X 8HB

Simon & Schuster Australia, Sydney

Simon & Schuster India, New Delhi

A CIP catalogue record for this book is available from the British Library.

ISBN 978-0-85707-880-3

Printed and bound in Great Britain by CPI Group (UK) Ltd, Croydon, CR0 4YY

www.simonandschuster.co.uk
www.simonandschuster.com.au
www.spellsisters.co.uk

AMBER CASTLE

Spell Sisters

ISABELLA
THE BUTTERFLY SISTER

Illustrations by Mary Hall

SIMON & SCHUSTER

Silver Hill

Croxton Manor

Morgana's Lair

Avalon

St Stephen's Church

Fairview Vineyard

Woolston Manor

Sunnyvale

Clement Castle

Halston Castle

Glendale Stables

Belleview
Bridge

N

Spell
Sisters

Spell Sisters

In a Forest Clearing

Morgana Le Fay stood in the opening of an enormous hollowed-out tree. Her long dark hair fell to her waist, and her skin was pale as moonlight. A raven was perched high in the branches, watching her with its beady black eyes.

'See what I can do, my beauty!' breathed Morgana. She pointed at the ground and clicked her fingers. The fallen leaves around her feet began to shake and tremble as large, long-legged black spiders scuttled out from the surrounding trees, drawn by her magic. They came from everywhere – dropping from branches on slivers of thread, running down tree trunks, gathering around her like a moving black carpet of crawling servants.

'Behold!' Morgana cried, laughing cruelly. 'All insects now move to my will!' She clicked her fingers again and a large fly appeared in front of the raven's beak.

The raven opened its beak and snapped the fly up.

Morgana chuckled. The raven flapped its wings and flew down to her shoulder with an appreciative caw.

'Now I must see what is going on. Show me the meddling girls!' Morgana hissed, pointing at the spiders. They swarmed around her bare feet, forming a picture. It showed two girls. One girl had red hair and was holding a harp. The other had blonde hair and held a flute to her mouth.

'Ridiculous children!' Morgana snarled, her expression darkening as she looked at the girls. 'They shall not stop me. Soon the island of Avalon will be mine! These girls may have freed two of the Spell Sisters of Avalon but the remaining six are still imprisoned, and while they are trapped, their powers belong to me! By the time of the next lunar eclipse, the Lady of the Lake's magic will no longer be able to prevent me from crossing to the island of Avalon and taking it for my own.' Her jet-black eyes glittered as she caressed the raven's feathers. 'I shall rule Avalon and bring destruction to this kingdom. All who hear my name shall fear me!'

Looking down at the spiders now starting

to scuttle over her bare feet, Morgana's mouth twisted into a triumphant smile. . .

Practice Makes Perfect

'Oh, I just can't do this!' Gwen exclaimed. Standing up, she put the small harp down crossly. 'I'm useless at playing music.'

Her cousin Flora lowered the flute she was playing. 'Gwen, you're not useless. You just need to practise more.'

'Practise, practise, practise! I'm bored of practising!' exclaimed Gwen. Shaking back her mane of red hair, she went to the narrow window of the guest bedchamber in Croxton Manor. The autumn sun was shining and she could see the trees with their golden and red leaves in the orchard beyond. She felt like she could almost smell the scent of ripe apples and woodsmoke in the air. 'I want to go out exploring,' she said longingly.

Outside the window there was a whole new world ripe for discovery. Croxton Manor belonged to Flora and Gwen's aunt and uncle. The girls had arrived, along with Flora's mother, a few hours ago. They were visiting to celebrate cousin Bethany's sixteenth birthday, and were staying for two nights. When they arrived in the carriage, Gwen had noticed beehives and a millpond, kennels and stables. She was itching to go out and look at everything properly.

'We can't go out. Mother said we have to rehearse our song for the party tonight,' Flora reminded her.

'Oh, it's not fair. Why do we have to be the ones to entertain everyone anyway?' groaned Gwen. 'It's a stupid idea.'

Flora smoothed down her sapphire-blue dress, a colour that perfectly matched the colour of her wide-set eyes. 'You know we have to play tonight. It's cousin Bethany's birthday, and Mother asked us especially. She will be really cross with us if we don't play the song well in front of everyone – we're representing her household. And you know Bethany will be upset too. Please, Gwen, come on. I really want her to be happy; it's her special day.'

Gwen rolled her eyes. 'I honestly don't know why you want to please Bethany so much. All she ever does is sit around reading silly poems about love and sighing over boys.'

'No she doesn't,' Flora protested.

'She does. And she hardly pays us any attention at all,' said Gwen.

Flora sighed dreamily. 'She's just so pretty and elegant and lady-like. I want to be like her when I'm older. Do you think I will be?'

'I hope not!' Gwen snorted. 'You'll be very boring if you are!'

'Bethany's not boring,' protested Flora.

'She is!' Gwen pushed a hand through her hair, which hung loosely at her shoulders. She never plaited it or wasted time putting ribbons in. It was tiresome enough having to comb it through each morning.

Sometimes Gwen really wished she could behave more like the boys at the castle. They didn't have to worry about their hair, and they had so much more fun! The boys were allowed to learn how to fight with swords and wrestle and joust on horseback, but girls were supposed to spend most of their time doing things like helping the older ladies in the family dress and do their hair, and learning how to run a household. Still, at least she was also allowed to go riding and to learn how to shoot with a bow and arrow. They were Gwen's two favourite things!

'I'm going to be *nothing* like Bethany when I'm sixteen,' she declared to Flora. 'When I'm grown-up, I'm going to spend all my time out riding and doing archery practice. I'm not going to sit around staring out of the window, thinking of meeting a husband and stroking my little lapdogs. I suppose I just can't understand why you'd want to be like Bethany, that's all.'

'Well, I do,' Flora said stubbornly. 'And I want to make her birthday special. Please, Gwen, just play the song again with me.'

Gwen looked into her cousin's pleading face. Flora was so different to her. Even though they always had good fun when they went on adventures together, Flora still loved being good and behaving like the perfect young lady, whereas Gwen just couldn't see the point. That day Flora's dress was spotless, and her long blonde braids were carefully decorated with silver thread to match the silver girdle she wore around her waist; Gwen took no such trouble with her appearance.

Gwen sighed. She was longing to go outside, she didn't care if they got into trouble for not practising, but she didn't want to upset Flora. They may have liked very different things, but the girls were the best of friends and Flora could be great fun when she stopped worrying about being lady-like.

'All right, come on,' Gwen said reluctantly. 'Let's practise some more then.'

Flora readied herself with her flute and Gwen picked up her harp, but as she did so, the large ocean-blue pendant she wore around her neck on a silver chain fell forward and bumped against the carved wooden top of the harp. Reaching for the

pendant to tuck it into the top of her dress, Gwen's thoughts were filled with a picture of Nineve, the beautiful young woman with long chestnut-brown hair whom she and Flora had met on the day they had found the necklace at the Lake surrounding the magical island of Avalon.

Gwen's brow wrinkled, and she looked over at her cousin. 'Flora,' she said, putting her harp down again. 'What will we do if Nineve calls us to go to the Lake while we're here?'

'I've been thinking about that too,' said Flora, looking worried. 'I don't know what we'd do. Hopefully she won't need us until we're home again. It's only a few days.'

When Gwen had first seen the pendant, its chain had been trapped inside a rock at the edge of the Lake. She had pulled the necklace free, and then to her and Flora's amazement, Nineve had risen up through the water by magic. She had told the girls that she was the Lady of the Lake, and that Avalon was in grave danger. The evil sorceress Morgana Le Fay had captured her eight sisters who lived on the island, stolen their magical powers and imprisoned them in different places all around the kingdom.

'I wonder if Morgana has tried to get to the island again,' Gwen said, thinking about the time they had been at the Lake and Morgana Le Fay had tried to cross it. The sorceress hadn't managed to reach the island, but it had been very scary. If she succeeded in her plan to take over Avalon, the consequences for the kingdom could be very grave.

Flora shivered. 'I really hope not.'

The Lady of the Lake had cast a spell on the water, making it impossible for Morgana to reach the island – but the spell would only last until the next lunar eclipse. All eight Spell Sisters had to be freed by then, or Morgana would return to the island and make it hers alone. Nineve had explained to Gwen and Flora that it was written in the stars that the human girl who could pull the pendant from the rock would be able to help. Gwen had been eager to help stop Morgana, and Flora had vowed to help too. So far they had released two of the sisters, Sophia and Lily, who had restored the power of fire and of plants back to the island. Gwen had been so pleased to see them back on Avalon where they belonged. Nineve had promised she would contact Gwen through the pendant as soon as she knew where another Spell Sister was trapped.

Gwen felt torn. 'I really want Nineve to contact us as soon as possible,' she said. 'I want to help her and the sisters – and have another adventure, of course! It just feels like every day that goes by when we don't find another sister means Morgana Le Fay is getting closer to taking over Avalon.'

Flora nodded, her brow creased with worry.

'But then again,' Gwen continued, 'if she does get in touch while we're all the way out here at Croxton Manor it would be so difficult to get to the Lake.'

'I suppose we'd better hope she doesn't contact us until we get home,' Flora said sensibly.

Gwen nodded. She knew Flora was right, but there was a bit of her that couldn't help secretly longing for another adventure that very second!

'But for the time being, seeing as we're here, we should practise our music,' Flora continued with a smile, giving Gwen a playful nudge.

So they started to play again. Gwen managed to focus on her harp playing for a few minutes, but then her thoughts started to drift towards Avalon once more. The magical island had once looked beautiful and green, covered with apple trees that bore fruit all year round, but since the Spell Sisters had been taken away, it had become barren and bare, the apple trees dying.

We've got to stop Morgana, Gwen thought. *The eclipse must be getting closer every day...*

Gwen's fingers stumbled distractedly on the strings of the harp.

'Gwen!' Flora exclaimed in frustration. 'You're not concentrating!'

Just as she spoke, the door to their chamber opened. A tall woman with blonde hair looked in. She was wearing a long green gown decorated with gold embroidery and her hair was coiled into a neat bun at the nape of her neck and held in place by a gold hairnet. It was Flora's mother, Gwen's Aunt Matilda. 'Hello, my dears. Have you got your new dresses ready for tonight?'

'Yes, Mother,' Flora answered meekly.

'And how is the practising going? We're all very much looking forward to hearing you both play later.'

Gwen and Flora exchanged looks. 'I think we need to work on the song a little bit more until it's perfect, Mother,' admitted Flora.

'Well, the chamber servant needs to come in now and clean the room, so why don't you bring your instruments downstairs and play them in the sitting room?' her mother suggested.

'Do we have to?' asked Gwen, a sinking feeling in her stomach. Other people might be in the sitting room, and she didn't want anyone to listen to them practising.

Aunt Matilda lifted her eyebrows. 'That is not the response I expect from a young lady, Guinevere.'

Gwen bit her lip. Her aunt insisted on complete obedience at all times. 'I beg your pardon, Aunt Matilda. Of course we will practise downstairs if you wish it,' she said politely.

Aunt Matilda smiled. 'That is better, child. Come now.'

She held the door open and ushered the girls

out with their instruments. She sailed down the stairs in front of them, her dress billowing around her. Flora tried to copy her mother's graceful movements, but tripped on the top step. Gwen grabbed her arm and stopped her falling. 'Be careful!' she said.

'Oh, I wish I wasn't always so clumsy!' exclaimed Flora. 'Young ladies are supposed to be elegant.'

'What *are* you going to do?' Gwen's green eyes danced teasingly. 'No one is *ever* going to want to marry you, Flora! You'll have to sit at a window and sigh as you read love poems, just like Bethany!'

Flora pushed her lightly. 'That's not funny! It's not nice to make fun of people.'

Gwen grinned, and her cousin couldn't help but return her smile.

'Girls!' Aunt Matilda glanced up from the bottom of the staircase looking irritated. 'Hurry up, please!'

Gwen and Flora ran down the stairs obediently to join her, carrying their instruments. Gwen really hoped *something* exciting would happen soon, otherwise today would be a real disappointment!

2
A Welcome Surprise

Croxton Manor was built on two floors. On the ground floor was a kitchen, a small chapel, a hall, and between the hall and the chapel, a sitting room.

The girls went in and looked at the tapestries hanging on the walls, and the warm fire burning in the large stone fireplace. Gwen's heart sank as she saw Bethany sitting beside the window.

She was gazing out, like a wistful princess, a book of love poems on her knee. Her two fluffy white dogs, Sugar and Spice, were curled up on embroidered cushions by the fire. Gwen usually liked all animals, but she found Bethany's dogs a little annoying. All they did was lie by the fire or sit on Bethany's knee – Gwen liked dogs who enjoyed a bit more rough and tumble, who wanted to play and go outside. She supposed these dogs were a lot like their owner. . .

'Now, girls, you start practising and I'll be back in a little while,' said Aunt Matilda from the doorway and she left the room.

'Hello, Bethany,' Flora said shyly.

Bethany didn't answer, but just carried on staring out of the window, her fingers twisting a strand of blonde hair that had come down from her bun. She sighed and put a hand to her heart.

'Oh dear. Why oh why does it hurt so much?'

Gwen knew she was trying to sound girly and romantic. She grinned to herself. 'Have you got a pain, Bethany?' she said, her green eyes wide. 'Something to do with your digestion maybe? I can always go to the kitchen and see if I can find some herbs. My mother swears by chewing a handful of dandelion leaves or. . .'

'Gwen, shh,' Flora said, frowning. 'Bethany's just thinking, aren't you, Bethany?'

'Yes, I am, dear one,' said Bethany, smiling at Flora. 'I am thinking many deep thoughts.'

'What about?' Flora breathed, going closer.

'About *love*, of course. About the knight who will one day come and claim me for his own. About the castle I shall live in and the life I shall lead. . .'

'Oh,' sighed Flora longingly.

'I'm thinking deep thoughts too,' put in Gwen.

'Really?' Bethany looked at her in surprise.

'Yes. I'm thinking about what's for dinner,' Gwen grinned. 'I'm really hungry!'

Bethany turned away in annoyance. Flora glared at Gwen for teasing her cousin. Grinning to herself, Gwen went to the fireplace and stroked the two dogs. They wagged their tails and she tickled them under their chins.

'We should practise our music,' said Flora. Gwen sat down on a chair with her harp, and Flora went to stand beside her, holding her flute up to her mouth.

They started well, but as Flora blew a string of high notes, the two little dogs jumped up from the cushions and began to yap. The girls glanced at each other, but carried on playing. The dogs

started to bark and
growl, backing away
towards the door.

'What a noise!'
exclaimed Bethany,
throwing her hands
in the air.

The door opened
and Aunt Matilda
came in. 'Goodness me!' she exclaimed. 'Stop,
girls! Stop!'

Gwen and Flora broke off from their
playing, and the dogs finally stopped yapping.

'Oh dear, maybe practising in here isn't such
a good idea,' Aunt Matilda said, shaking her
head.

'Yes indeed, Aunty,' Bethany said quickly.
'Sugar and Spice really don't seem to like it. And

it's giving me such a headache as well! I need to rest before the party tonight!'

Aunt Matilda glanced out of the window. 'I have an idea, girls. It's dry outside at the moment, so why don't you go and practise in the rose garden instead? You shouldn't cause too much of a disturbance out there.'

Gwen's heart leaped. It would be *much* more fun being outside, even if they did still have to practise their song! 'Of course, Aunt Matilda,' she replied, not finding it at all hard to be obedient this time. 'Come along, Flora! Young ladies should always obey their elders, remember?' She gave her cousin an innocent look.

Flora rolled her eyes. 'Bye, Bethany,' she said. 'See you later on for the party!'

'Goodbye, my dear,' smiled Bethany.

Gwen pulled Flora out of the room. 'Take

care, *my dear*,' she whispered teasingly as the door shut behind them. 'Come and get your outdoor cloak, *my dear*.'

Flora gave her a cross look. 'Be quiet.'

Gwen grinned. 'Sorry. Bethany's just so dull! Come on, let's go outside.'

They hurried back to their chamber to put on their thick woollen outdoor cloaks – although it was sunny outside, there was a chill to the autumn air. Gwen fastened the iron brooch that held her dark green cloak in place and pulled on her boots. 'Hurry up!' she urged Flora who was busy checking her reflection in the looking glass.

'Young ladies should learn to be patient!' Flora retorted. Gwen pulled a face at her. Flora grinned, and they made their way outside.

The rose garden was in one corner of the main garden and the bushes were arranged in a

pattern of square beds. Many of the flowers had faded now and large rose hips were forming, but there were still a few yellow and white blooms on branches that arched over to the ground. Gwen breathed in deeply. It was lovely to be out of the stuffy manor house and into the fresh autumn air.

'Let's go and explore,' she said, putting her

harp down on a nearby bench. 'I want to go and see the stables and the barns.'

'I don't know, Gwen. We're meant to be rehearsing our song. . .' Flora said cautiously.

'Come on, Flora. We could explore for just for a few minutes, couldn't we?' Gwen looked at her pleadingly.

'But what if Mother comes to check on us?' Flora pointed out. 'No. We can't. We—' She broke off with a gasp and pointed at Gwen.

Gwen frowned. 'What is it?' She glanced down, wondering if she had something on her dress or cloak, and then she gasped too.

The magic pendant around her neck was sparkling with a silvery light!

Nineve's Message

Gwen grasped the pendant with trembling fingers and held it up to see properly. A mist was swirling over its blue surface. As the mist cleared, the beautiful face of Nineve, the Lady of the Lake, was revealed in the depths of the stone.

'Guinevere,' Nineve whispered, seeming to look straight from the pendant deep into Gwen's eyes.

Gwen felt excitement surge through her. Her fingers tightened on the pendant. 'Yes, Nineve! Do you need us? Have you found another Spell Sister?'

'I have.' Nineve's voice was soft and musical. 'I have seen where Isabella, the Spell Sister with the power over all insects, is trapped. Come to the Lake and I will show you what my magic has revealed.'

Gwen glanced at Flora, who was peering over her shoulder. What were they going to do? How *could* they go? They were miles from the Lake.

'Will you come now, my friends?' urged Nineve.

'Oh, Nineve,' Gwen said. 'We're not at Halston Castle, we're at another house quite far away. Even if we could get to the Lake, we wouldn't be back until very late, and there's a big celebration here tonight that we have to go to.'

'Oh dear, what unfortunate timing! I fear Isabella may be in grave danger and really needs your help. . .' said Nineve.

Gwen felt awful. How could she go to a party when one of the Spell Sisters needed her? She made up her mind. She couldn't. 'All right! We'll come!' she declared.

'Gwen, how can we do that?' said Flora, looking at her friend with concern.

Gwen stood her ground. 'We'll see you soon, Nineve.'

'I will be waiting,' said Nineve, smiling. 'Thank you so much, girls!' The mist swirled across the pendant again and her image vanished.

Gwen turned to Flora, who was staring at her as if she was mad.

'Why did you tell Nineve we'd go? We can't. How would we get there and back in time?' Flora said.

'We have to try,' replied Gwen. 'Isabella needs us. Don't you want to help?'

'Of *course* I do.' Flora seemed to be wavering the more she thought about it. 'It would be wonderful to have another adventure, and I really want to help. It's just the party is tonight, and everyone will be so worried if we're not here.

It will ruin Bethany's birthday. We can't do that.'

Gwen bit her lip. She might not like Bethany much, but she didn't want to spoil her celebration, or make people worry about them. What could they do? *Oh, if only we could get to the Lake quickly and find out where Isabella is, but still be back in time to play our instruments,* she thought, *but how can we* possibly *do that?*

A picture of a pure white horse filled her mind. 'If only we had Moonlight with us here!' she cried.

Moonlight was a wild stallion that Gwen and Flora had found in the forest during their first adventure. Gwen had fed him an apple from Avalon which had tamed him and given him the power to gallop incredibly fast. It also meant he could understand where the girls needed to go and what they wanted him to do. If only he was nearby, they would be able to race to the Lake and back in no time at all. Gwen's fingers closed around the pendant again. *Oh, Moonlight,* she thought desperately, *I really wish you were here!*

A sharp tingle jumped through her hands. Gwen dropped the pendant in surprise.

'What's the matter?' said Flora, noticing Gwen's startled expression.

'I. . . I felt something strange,' Gwen stammered. 'It was like a shock or something ran through my fingers from the pendant. I was just thinking about Moonlight, wishing he was here, and. . . ' Gwen broke off as a faint whinny rang through the air.

'What was that?' said Flora.

Gwen caught her breath. Surely it couldn't be Moonlight, could it?

The girls heard the sound of galloping

hooves getting closer and closer. A few seconds later, a white stallion came soaring over the wall of the manor house garden. He raced across the grass towards them.

'It's Moonlight!' cried Gwen in astonishment. 'He must have got here by magic!'

Flora gaped, her mouth opening and shutting like one of the golden carp in the fishpond. 'B-but what if someone sees him!' she stammered. 'Gwen! We'll be in so much trouble! He can't be here. He just can't!'

'Well, he is!' Gwen laughed.

Moonlight stopped and shook back his long mane. Throwing her arms round his neck, Gwen cried: 'Oh, Moonlight, it's so good to see you!'

The horse neighed softly and nuzzled her shoulder.

'Gwen!' Flora exclaimed, looking around

frantically. 'One of the servants could come out at any moment. Or Mother might come looking for us.'

'Then let's get out of here!' said Gwen. 'Will you take us to the Lake, Moonlight?'

Moonlight whinnied and stamped a front hoof.

Gwen chuckled. 'I think that means yes!' Taking hold of Moonlight's mane, she hitched up her skirts and vaulted on to his back. She was very athletic and an experienced rider, although the ponies she normally rode at the castle were nothing like the beautiful stallion. But Gwen was getting used to riding him now. 'Let's go, Flora!'

She saw Flora hesitate. 'It will be all right, I promise!' Gwen urged. 'We'll be back as soon as we can. You know how fast Moonlight can gallop.' She looked pleadingly at her cousin. 'Please, Flora. Avalon's depending on us!'

Flora pushed her flute into the pocket of her dress. 'Very well,' she said with a smile. 'But what about your harp, Gwen?'

'It'll have to stay here. I can't take it with me,' said Gwen.

'We should hide it, just in case Mother does

come out.' Flora tucked it down behind the bench in the long grass. 'We can always say we moved on somewhere else to practise.' Then, taking hold of Gwen's hand, Flora scrambled behind her on to Moonlight's back.

Gwen waited until Flora was settled and then clapped her heels to Moonlight's  sides. With a joyful whinny, the stallion set off. He cantered straight towards the garden wall.

'H-he's going awfully fast,' Flora said nervously.

'He's got to get up some speed so we can jump!' Gwen called.

'Jump? Can't we go through the gates? Gwen, I've never jumped before!' Flora squealed as the red bricks loomed in front of them.

'Just hang on tight!' shouted Gwen. The wall came closer. Gwen felt Moonlight gather himself. As he leaped upwards, Flora shrieked and shut her eyes, but Gwen whooped in delight. It was like flying!

The stallion landed safely on the other side.

'Oh my goodness! Oh my goodness!' gasped Flora, gripping Gwen's waist. 'I feel sick!'

'Go, Moonlight!' Gwen cried to the horse. 'Gallop as fast as you can!'

Moonlight raced away, streaking past the strips of land planted with crops and the occasional small stone cottage, and then galloping across the rough heathland, past streams and bushes, until he came to the forest. He plunged into the cool darkness of the trees, his hooves sending flurries of fallen leaves up into the air. Gwen breathed

in the damp scent of leaf mould and ivy. It was wonderful to be in the forest again! She ducked close to Moonlight's neck to avoid the low branches as he twisted and turned through the tree trunks.

At last, the stallion came to a halt. Sitting up, Gwen saw that they had reached the Lake. Its still surface was as smooth as glass. A purple mist swirled over the centre, hiding the island of Avalon.

Gwen scrambled off Moonlight's back and reached up to help Flora down.

Flora's face was pale. 'That was *very* fast.'

'I loved it! Thank you, boy,' Gwen said, stroking Moonlight's warm neck. Then they hurried over the rocks at the water's edge. 'Nineve!' Gwen called. 'We're here.'

She and Flora watched as a single ripple ran

across the silvery surface of the Lake, and then the waters parted and Nineve rose up through them. Her hair was caught off her face with a headband made of tiny pearls, and her blue-green robes shimmered. 'Guinevere! Flora!' she greeted them warmly. 'Thank heavens you were able to come!'

Nineve ran across the water, her bare feet hardly seeming to touch the surface. She stopped at the very edge of the Lake, but took care not to leave it. 'I am very glad to see you both!'

Gwen knew that if Nineve stepped out of the Lake, then the magic spell that kept Morgana from crossing to the island would be broken. 'We came as quickly as we could,' Gwen said.

'It's lovely to see you, Nineve,' added Flora.

The Lady of the Lake smiled. 'Thank you both for coming with such speed. I really do hope your being here will not cause you to get into trouble. Are you ready to see where the third Spell Sister of Avalon is trapped?'

'Oh, yes!' breathed Gwen and Flora.

Searching for Isabella

Nineve raised both hands above her head and then clasped her fingers lightly together. Gwen and Flora watched eagerly – twice now Nineve had shown them images on the surface of the Lake. How would she do it this time?

Nineve whispered a word and then slowly brought her hands down and opened them up. Gwen and Flora gasped as they saw a delicate dragonfly sitting on Nineve's palms, its transparent wings shimmering, its body a bright green-blue.

Nineve leaned closer to it. 'Will you show us where Isabella is trapped, please, my friend?' she whispered.

The dragonfly flew upwards and darted around Nineve's head, a shimmer of sparkling colour. It skimmed briefly across the Lake just in front of the girls. Its wings whirred, and as the water rippled, an image formed on the surface. The dragonfly circled in the air and Gwen and Flora saw an image clearly on the Lake. It showed the outside of a cave. There were tall trees surrounding it.

'That is where I believe Isabella is,' said Nineve. 'I think she is trapped in that cave somehow, and while she remains there, Morgana has the use of her powers and can control all the insects in the land.'

'But where is the cave?' asked Flora. 'Do you know, Nineve?'

Nineve shook her head. 'No, I'm sorry, I'm afraid I do not. You must discover that for yourselves.'

'I've never seen a cave like it before,' said Gwen. 'Though the trees make it look as if it might be in the forest somewhere.'

'But the forest is so big,' said Flora. 'How will we find it? We could be searching for weeks!'

Gwen looked at Nineve. 'I wish I could help you look,' Nineve said sadly, 'but, as you know, I must stay here in the Lake or the enchantment will break.'

The image of the cave slowly started to fade from the water.

'What can we do?' Flora said to Gwen.

'I don't know. It's really tricky to think how to find the cave without knowing where to even start,' Gwen said, rubbing her forehead in frustration. But she wasn't going to give up so easily. She couldn't bear the thought of going back without looking for Isabella at all. If only they knew where the cave was, then they could get to it quickly and try to free her.

The dragonfly flew from Nineve's hand where it had settled again, and began to circle Gwen's head. Gwen gently waved it away. She needed to concentrate. How could they find out where the cave was? There had to be a way.

Think, she muttered to herself. *Think*.

The dragonfly dodged her hand and instead fluttered down and hovered in front of her face. Gwen looked at it and felt her skin prickle. She suddenly had a feeling that it was trying to tell her something. 'What is it?' she said curiously to the insect.

The dragonfly moved up and down slightly, and then zipped past her and headed towards the trees. It stopped and turned back, as if waiting for her. 'I think it wants us to follow it!' said Gwen.

'What? The dragonfly?' Flora looked surprised.

'Yes!' Gwen's heart thudded with excitement. She was sure the little insect wanted them to go with it. She took a step towards the dragonfly and it flew on a little more before stopping. 'I think it knows the way to the cave,' she said. 'Let's get on Moonlight and follow it!'

'Wait a moment, Gwen,' Flora said, backing away from the dragonfly. 'What if it's a trap? We know Morgana controls all the insects now – she could be using this one to lead us into danger.' She glanced at Nineve to see what she thought.

'A good point,' Nineve agreed. 'But Morgana cannot control *this* dragonfly because he came forth from my magic.' The Lady of the Lake studied the sparkling creature, who was still hovering in wait, his wings a blur of silver. 'I think Guinevere is right. Perhaps he will indeed be able to lead the way to the cave. Magic works in mysterious ways. Isabella will still retain traces of her ability even though she is imprisoned. The dragonfly may feel a connection with her.'

'Let's follow him then!' Gwen said eagerly. 'After all, what have we got to lose? We've got no other clues.'

Flora nodded, trusting her friend's instincts. 'You're right – it's worth a try. Let's see where it takes us.' They both ran towards Moonlight.

'Good luck, my friends!' called Nineve, waving her hand. 'May the magic of Avalon speed you on your way.'

Gwen and Flora mounted Moonlight, and the stallion followed the dragonfly swiftly. The insect headed to the east, leading them into a part of the forest Gwen had never been to before. The trees were tall and clustered closely together, their twisted branches catching at Moonlight's mane and tail as they passed. The ground grew boggier under the horse's hooves. His canter slowed to a trot and then a walk, as he had to pick his way

dragonfly darted ahead of them, a glimmer in the gloom.

'I don't like it here,' said Flora, shivering as she looked at the trees pressing in around them.

'Me neither,' said Gwen.

Moonlight stopped suddenly, giving a snort. There was a large patch of boggy ground covering the path ahead. Around the edge of it was a little bank but it was too narrow for Moonlight to walk on. The horse cautiously stepped out with one front hoof. It squelched down on the black surface and his leg sank in all the way to the knee. Moonlight snorted in alarm and pulled back.

'Steady, boy,' Gwen soothed, stroking his neck. 'He's not going to be able to get through,' she said over her shoulder to Flora. 'It's a sinking bog.' Gwen had spent enough time in the forest around the castle to know that you had to be very careful with sinking bogs. They looked just like normal mud

on the path, but if you tried to walk through them, your feet would sink and they would suck you slowly in. Escaping was really difficult no matter how much you struggled and fought to get free. She had heard all sorts of stories about people and animals who had tried to walk through the bogs and never returned.

Moonlight stamped his foot and whinnied anxiously.

'Maybe we should try and find another way round it,' suggested Flora.

Gwen looked at the dragonfly waiting for them on the other side of the bog. 'We can't follow you this way!' she called to it. But the dragonfly didn't seem to understand and just darted further along the path.

'We're going to lose him!' Flora said urgently.

'There's only one thing for it,' said Gwen

quickly. 'We'll have to leave Moonlight here. We can get round the bog if we climb on to the bank. He'll be fine on his own; there's water and grass for him and hopefully we'll be back soon.'

They dismounted. 'Wait here for us,' Gwen told the stallion. 'We'll be back as soon as we can.'

Moonlight whinnied anxiously as if warning them to be careful.

Gwen stepped on to the bank and edged cautiously round the bog. She used the tree trunks and branches, hanging on to them as her feet slipped on the muddy ground. Flora followed slowly, trying her best to copy Gwen's movements. Gwen kept a watchful eye on her cousin. Now would not be a good time for one of Flora's clumsy moments!

Gwen was very relieved when they both made it safely on to the other side. She took one last look back at Moonlight, who had started to graze on the few tufts of grass at his feet, and then ran after the dragonfly as it flew once more along the overgrown path.

Gwen leaped easily over the tree roots and brambles, but Flora started to fall behind as they raced through the forest.

'Here, Flora, hold my hand and let me help you!' Gwen said, glancing around and seeing her cousin was lagging some way back.

Flora shook her head. 'I can manage on my own. I'm just trying to be careful so I don't get my dress dirty or torn. If we come back to the party all filthy then Mother and Bethany will certainly know we've been up to something.'

'But if you don't go any faster, then we'll lose the dragonfly,' Gwen urged as Flora caught up with her. 'Come on, just grab hold of my hand,

Flora. I'll make sure you don't fall.'

'No, I'm fine!' Flora insisted. She overtook Gwen. 'I don't need any help. . . See, I'm— whaaa!' she squealed as she tripped over a tree root and fell over, landing on all fours with a thud.

'Are you all right?' Gwen hurried to help Flora out.

'Oh no! I'm covered in mud!' Flora said, standing up, her skirt dripping wet.

Gwen spotted Flora's flute on the ground – it had fallen out of her pocket. Picking it up, she wiped it clean on her cloak and handed it to Flora. 'Here.'

'Thanks,' sighed Flora. She thrust the flute into her pocket again. As she did so, her eyes caught Gwen's and she couldn't help herself – she started to giggle. 'So much for keeping my dress clean!'

Seeing that Flora was giggling, Gwen began to laugh too. 'I don't *need* any help. . . whaaa!' she teased, mimicking her friend.

They both chuckled. 'Oh, I wish I was as good at running and climbing and doing outdoors stuff as you,' Flora sighed.

Gwen took her hand. 'You just need more practise.'

Flora raised her eyebrows. 'But Gwen, I thought you said practising was boring – that's what you told me back at the manor house.'

'Very funny!' said Gwen, returning her

cousin's grin. 'Come on, we'd better get going – we need to keep up!'

They went on following the dragonfly, trying not to let it dart too far ahead of them. It was hard – they had to go as fast as they could. After five minutes, they reached another bog. Gwen threw a rock in and watched it sink without trace. 'Be very careful!' she warned Flora. 'It seems even deeper than the first one.'

They made their way around it, being sure to only stand on firm ground at the very edge, but when they reached the other side, Flora stopped. 'I'm so tired,' she said, wiping her brow. 'Do you think we're almost. . .?' She broke off as a low snarl rumbled suddenly through the air. 'Gwen, did you hear that. . .? What was that?' she stammered, the colour draining out of her face.

Gwen looked around. There was another

snarl, and then another. A shiver ran down her spine, and she studied the treeline closely. Then, to her horror, she caught sight of eight shadows the size of very large dogs, stalking through the trees towards them. 'Wolves. . .!' she whispered, feeling as if a bucket of icy water had just been poured over her.

Flora gripped her arm, her eyes wide with fear.

Gwen had never run into wolves in the forest before, but she'd heard that some of them did roam in the lonelier areas. She and Flora froze for a moment as they saw the creatures emerge from the shadows of the trees. The leader of the wolf pack was bulky and powerful, his fur shaggy and grey.

Gwen automatically reached for her bow and arrows, but then realised with a sick feeling that she didn't have them with her – they were still back at the manor house. They had been in such a hurry to leave that she hadn't picked them up. She and Flora were facing eight wolves with nothing to defend themselves with.

The leader of the wolves came closer, his

yellow eyes fixed menacingly on them. Gwen was suddenly reminded of watching a cat stalking a mouse in the castle stables. The wolf snarled again, and the sound almost seemed to make the ground shake it was so fierce.

Flora trembled. 'Wh-what are we going to do, Gwen?'

Gwen swallowed. She had absolutely no idea.

A Narrow Escape

The leading wolf crouched down and stared at Gwen and Flora, readying himself to spring, and the others prowled closer behind him.

Be brave, Gwen told herself. She knew that most wild animals were more scared of humans than humans were of them, and if you acted confidently, they would usually run away.

Taking a deep breath, she threw back

her shoulders and marched towards the wolves, raising her arms. 'Go on! Away with you!' she shouted loudly. 'Go on. Shoo!'

The wolf at the head of the pack raised his hackles and growled even more savagely. He didn't move away at all – none of the wolves seemed worried by her at all.

'Gwen! Be careful!' Flora exclaimed. 'What are you doing?'

'Trying to scare them,' replied Gwen.

'Well, it's not working!' Flora gasped as the wolves began to prowl even closer to them, snapping their jaws and moving as one, as if obeying a silent command only they could hear.

'But I don't understand. Wild animals are normally scared of humans,' Gwen said in confusion.

'Not these ones.' Flora gulped, staring at

the advancing wolves.

'It's like someone's telling them what to do!' Gwen said, her skin prickling.

Flora's blue eyes widened. 'Maybe it's Morgana! Could she be controlling them?'

Gwen's heart sank like a stone in a well. Of course! Morgana was bound to be trying to stop them from getting to the cave. Looking at the wolves gazing at them hungrily with unblinking eyes, she was sure Flora was right and that this was somehow Morgana's doing.

'What are we going to do?' whispered Flora.

Gwen's thoughts raced. What *could* they do? There were eight large wolves in front of them and a sinking bog behind. There didn't seem to be any way to escape.

The bog. . .

She caught her breath. 'Flora. I think I might

have a plan!' Gwen hissed as the wolves growled louder and snapped their sharp teeth together threateningly. 'There's no time to explain. Just do what I say and when I count to three – jump!'

'Jump where?' Flora cried.

'Don't worry, just follow my lead. Come on!' Gwen turned, grabbing Flora's hand, and began to run.

'What are you doing?' gasped Flora. 'The wolves are going to chase us!'

'That's the plan,' called Gwen grimly.

'But—'

Flora broke off, and Gwen saw the wolf leader start to spring. Gripping Flora's hand, she raced towards the bog, pulling her cousin with her. She heard snarling rumble out once more as all the wolves chased after them. They were fast and strong, and Gwen knew they would catch her and Flora in just a few paces. Her plan had better work! She could hear the wolves bearing down on them, feel their breath on her back, hear their snarls and growls. She and Flora were at the edge of the bog. It stretched out in front of them.

'One, two, three – JUMP!' yelled Gwen. She leaped into the air, pulling Flora with her. To her relief, her cousin jumped as well. They flew across the muddy ground and landed on

the other side, falling on their hands and knees. Gwen heard her dress rip, but that was the least of her worries. Scrambling up, she looked behind her. Had her plan worked?

Yes! Relief rushed over Gwen. The wolves had been so intent on chasing her and Flora that they hadn't seen the bog. They had run straight into it! The wolves were floundering, their legs sinking and their grey fur getting covered with

the dark mud from the bog as they howled and fought to get out.

'Quick!' Gwen shouted to Flora, realising there was no time to lose. 'Let's get out of here before they manage to free themselves.'

'But what about the dragonfly?' demanded Flora. 'We've lost it now!'

Gwen searched the air, desperately hoping to see the insect's fluttering wings. 'No we haven't. There it is!'

She pointed to the dragonfly hovering a short distance ahead of them. It seemed to realise that they couldn't continue the way they had been heading. Turning round, it darted off the path and lead them straight through the trees.

Gwen and Flora charged after it, with the wolves' howls still ringing in their ears. The dragonfly led them past hawthorn bushes and horse chestnut trees, through hazel groves and past an enormous oak tree, until finally they came to the edge of the forest and into a clearing. Then they saw it – a dark grey rocky cliff with a cave at its base.

'We're here!' exclaimed Gwen. 'That looks just like the cave we saw in the image on the Lake.'

'Oh, thank you!' Flora said to the little dragonfly. It flew down to her hand, bobbed its head at her and then darted away into the trees, its job now done.

The girls stared at the cave. It looked dark and shadowy and reminded Gwen of an open mouth waiting to be fed. She hesitated, suddenly not wanting to go closer. The sky was blue and the sun was shining, but she could feel icy pinpricks running all over her skin.

'It's strange here,' said Flora uneasily. 'It's very still, isn't it?'

Gwen nodded. She thought of the places they had rescued the first two Spell Sisters from. They'd had the same still, mysterious feeling in the air. However, she pushed her shoulders back. She and Flora had come this far. They weren't going to turn back now. If Isabella was trapped inside that cave, they were going to set her free!

Taking a deep breath, Gwen went over to the wide, rocky entrance. 'Hello?' she called. 'Is there anyone in there?'

There was no answer. Her voice echoed back at her.

'Isabella?' Gwen called again. She tried stepping inside the cave, but once she was past the gloomy light of the entrance, it was pitch-black inside. She couldn't see a thing in there. There was no knowing how far the cave went back or what was in there at all. She pulled back and turned to Flora in frustration. 'We need some light.'

'If only we had a lantern or a candle with us,' said Flora.

Gwen thought of her travelling bag back at Halston Castle. She had been keeping it specially packed for when they were next called on an adventure. There was a candle in it, and a tinderbox to light it with. She had thought she'd been really clever packing it and getting it ready, but what use was it back in their bedroom at home? Now they were going to have to just do the best they could without it.

'We'll have to *make* a torch,' Gwen said. 'Let's see.' She glanced around. Their friend Arthur, one of the pages at the castle, had once taught Gwen how to make a fire without a tinderbox. If she found a stick and some fabric, she could wrap the material around the stick and then set light to it, making it into a flaming torch. There were lots of sticks under the nearby trees. She spotted a perfect one on the ground and picked it up. But what about the fabric?

Looking down, Gwen's eyes fell on the ripped hem of her skirt. That would be perfect! She grabbed it and pulled hard. A long strip of material tore off in her hands revealing the bottom of her white undergown.

'Gwen!' Flora looked horrified. 'What are you doing?'

'Making a torch,' Gwen said, wrapping the strip of fabric around the stick and tying it tightly.

'But your dress! Mother will be furious when she sees it.'

'So?' At that moment, Aunt Matilda seemed a very long way away to Gwen. All she cared about was getting into the cave and having a look around to see if they could find Isabella.

It probably wasn't going to be easy. Morgana usually disguised the trapped sisters, transforming them into other things.

The stick was soon ready with the material bound tightly at the top. Now it just needed to be lit. Gwen knew she would need a piece of flint, some metal and some kindling that would catch fire easily. She hunted around, picking up some dried leaves, old dry moss and a bit of wool that seemed to have come from a bird's nest, then she picked up a piece of flint and sat down on the ground.

Flora watched in astonishment as Gwen took the iron brooch off her cloak, scrunched up the dry kindling and began to strike the flint hard against the brooch, aiming it towards the kindling. It took quite a few attempts, but then a spark jumped from the flint and flew into the ball of kindling. Gwen waited anxiously. After a few moments, a trickle of smoke rose into the air.

'It's working!' said Flora in awe. 'It's going to set the kindling alight.'

Gwen blew very gently and a small flame flickered into life, quickly eating up the dry wool and leaves. She picked up her makeshift torch from beside her and carefully used the flames to light the material around the end of the stick.

When she held it up, the end was burning like a giant candle. 'There!' she declared.

'You're so clever!' said Flora, impressed. 'I didn't even know you could make fire like that!'

'Arthur taught me. I'll have to say a big thank you to him when we get back,' said Gwen, getting to her feet. *If we get back*, she added silently to herself. They still had to find and rescue Isabella, and one thing she was sure of was that Morgana wasn't going to make it easy for them.

Holding the torch high, Gwen looked towards the cave. She knew the flames wouldn't last for long.

'Let's get moving!'

In the Cave

The girls cautiously entered the cave. The flaming torch that Gwen had made threw light all around, illuminating the gloom, but making the shadows at the back and sides of the rocky hollow seem even darker. The air in the cave felt as cold as a tomb. . . Gwen quickly squashed the thought, and swept the branch around, using the flames to light up the shadows. Where was Isabella?

'The wall at the back of the cave looks like it's glittering,' whispered Flora. 'Can you see it?'

Gwen saw that the back of the cave was indeed sparkling. Moving closer, she realised that the whole wall was studded with gleaming purple crystals. 'It's beautiful!' she said, holding the torch up and watching as the crystals glimmered in the light.

'There's a pattern,' said Flora suddenly. 'Sort of like a picture. Look!' She went closer and peered at the cave wall. 'Gwen! I think it's a girl!' Flora gently traced the pattern with her finger. 'Here's her head and body, arms and legs. Can you see it?'

Gwen realised that Flora was right. The crystals formed the image of a young woman. 'It has to be Isabella!' she said. 'Morgana must have trapped her in the wall. Oh, the poor thing!'

'Quick! Set her free!' Flora urged. 'Can you remember what to do, Gwen?'

'Of course.' Gwen wedged the flaming branch in a crack between two rocks and pulled the pendant out from under her cloak. Holding it firmly against the frozen image of the sister she began to chant the spell that would release Isabella:

'*Spell Sister of Avalon, I now . . .*'

'STOP!' A harsh voice rang out through the cave and echoed menacingly all around them.

Gwen's heart leaped into her throat. There was only one person that could be!

'It's Morgana,' Flora whispered in fear.

'You shall not break the enchantment,' the sorceress's voice snarled.

They looked around wildly. Where was her voice coming from?

'Look as hard as you like, but you will not see me. My magic is too powerful for the likes of you silly girls. Unlike you, I can see everything you are doing. You will not succeed!' Morgana Le Fay's voice echoed. 'I will stop you.'

'Oh, no you won't!' cried Gwen bravely.

'No!' joined in Flora. 'We're going to free Isabella!'

'Even if you free my sister, none of you shall

escape!' Morgana's laugh rang out metallically. 'You will all be trapped in here until you die! You will be sorry you ever decided to interfere with my plans!' She began to chant a spell:

'To make sure these girls will fail,
Rock and crystal, form a jail!'

There was a loud rumbling, grating sound. Flora grabbed Gwen's arm as the ground at the cave entrance started to move. 'What. . . what's happening?'

Gwen pulled Flora to the back of the cave as sharp points began to push upwards through the floor.

'Oh my goodness, Gwen! Look!' Flora cried, pointing up to the ceiling. Large icicle-like shapes made from rock were stabbing downwards

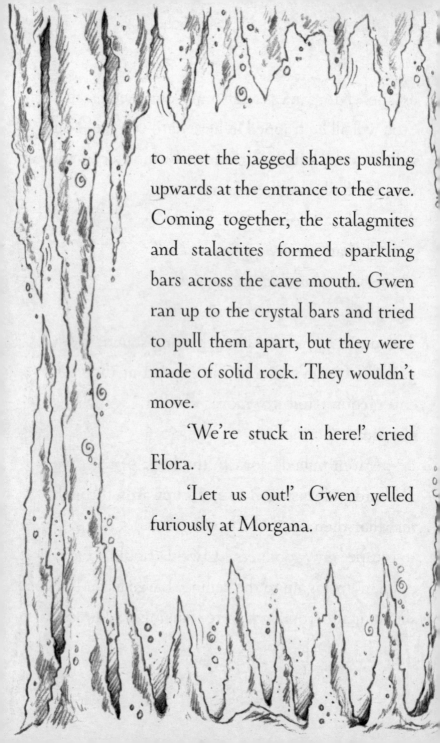

to meet the jagged shapes pushing upwards at the entrance to the cave. Coming together, the stalagmites and stalactites formed sparkling bars across the cave mouth. Gwen ran up to the crystal bars and tried to pull them apart, but they were made of solid rock. They wouldn't move.

'We're stuck in here!' cried Flora.

'Let us out!' Gwen yelled furiously at Morgana.

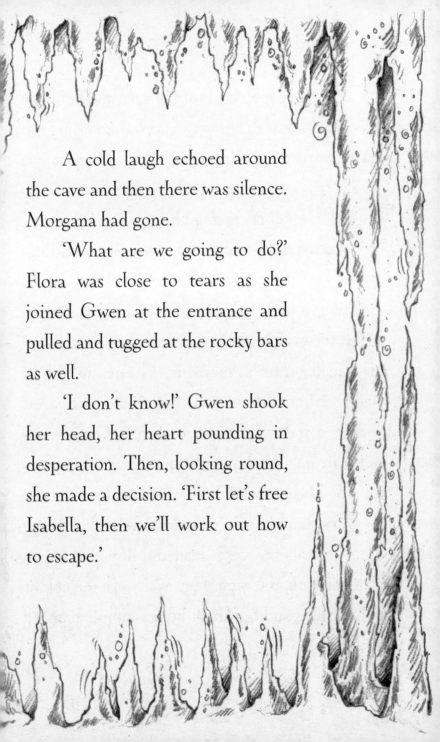

A cold laugh echoed around the cave and then there was silence. Morgana had gone.

'What are we going to do?' Flora was close to tears as she joined Gwen at the entrance and pulled and tugged at the rocky bars as well.

'I don't know!' Gwen shook her head, her heart pounding in desperation. Then, looking round, she made a decision. 'First let's free Isabella, then we'll work out how to escape.'

She ran to the back of the cave and held her pendant against the figure in crystal, chanting the magic words that Nineve had taught her:

'Spell Sister of Avalon I now release,
Return to the island and help bring peace.'

As the girls watched, a purple light slowly spread across the back of the cave, illuminating the shape of Isabella. For a moment, Gwen and Flora could see her outline growing clearer and clearer, and then the wall began to shiver. The crystals suddenly dissolved in a shimmer of sparkles, and the Spell Sister floated out of the rocky wall!

Gwen and Flora stared as she glided to the floor. Isabella was very small and slim, and only a little taller than Gwen. Her eyes were the colour of hazelnuts and her thick honey-blonde hair fell to her feet. She was wearing a dress that glowed all shades of amber and gold and she had a large diamond pendant in the shape of a dragonfly around her neck on a delicate gold chain.

'You've broken Morgana's enchantment!' she cried. 'I don't know how you did it, but thank you both! I am Isabella, one of the Spell Sisters of Avalon.'

'We know,' Gwen told her with a smile. 'Nineve sent us here to rescue you. I'm Guinevere, and this is Flora.'

'We've freed two of your sisters already – Sophia

and Lily,' put in Flora.

'Thank you. You are both very brave. But what about my other sisters?' Isabella asked anxiously. 'Where are they?'

'I'm afraid they're still imprisoned somewhere,' Gwen admitted. 'Morgana Le Fay has them scattered all over the kingdom.'

'And now we're trapped in here,' said Flora, pointing to the entrance. 'Morgana has used her magic. We can't get out.'

Isabella ran to the crystal bars. Her movements reminded Gwen of an insect – light and swift, her bare feet hardly seeming to touch the floor of the cave. 'Oh, if only I had power over minerals and rocks like my sister Amelia!' Isabella exclaimed in frustration. 'I could make these bars disappear with magic, and then we could escape.'

A thought came into Gwen's head. 'When we rescued your sisters, Sophia and Lily, they were able to magically transport themselves back to the Lake. Can't you escape like that, Isabella? You could get away from here.'

Isabella looked shocked. 'I could, but I'm not going to leave you two trapped here. I won't.'

'But if you went, you could get help,' Flora told her. 'Maybe Nineve would be able to do something.'

'But who knows what Morgana might do while I am gone. I won't go,' Isabella said stubbornly. 'You rescued me. I'm not going to desert you. I'm certain we can think of some way for us *all* to escape.'

Gwen and Flora exchanged looks. They couldn't force Isabella to return to Avalon without them, but what were they going to do?

Gwen wracked her brains. 'Maybe we could try and squeeze through the bars somehow,' she suggested, starting to examine all the gaps. There seemed to be a slightly larger space between two of the crystal icicles to the left-hand side. There *might* be just enough room there for them to get through. 'Do you think we could get through here, Flora?'

Flora came over and investigated. 'There might be enough room. Let me see.' Turning sideways, she started to squeeze herself through the tiny gap. She got one leg and a shoulder through, but her head simply wouldn't fit between the bars. 'There's not quite enough space,' she gasped. 'Just a little more room and. . .'

All of a sudden, a vicious growl came from outside the cave. Flora gave a squeak and pulled herself quickly back inside. Gwen's heart missed a beat. It couldn't be. . . could it?

She swallowed as eight dark shapes slipped like shadows between the tree trunks outside the cave. There was another loud snarl. It was the wolves from the forest! They prowled into the open, their thick coats now caked in mud. Their teeth were bared and their yellow eyes were gleaming hungrily.

7
Trapped!

'The wolves!' Gwen exclaimed in horror. 'They must have escaped from the bog and tracked us down!'

Bounding forward, the leader of the wolves sprang towards the cave entrance. The girls and Isabella jumped back as his powerful body crashed into the rocky bars. He snapped his jaws at them all, showing his pointed teeth. The rest of the pack joined him, throwing themselves over and over again at the barrier with vicious snarls and howls, and snapping at the girls between the bars. The noise echoed deafeningly around the cave.

'Why are they attacking us like this?' cried Isabella, backing away.

'We think they're under Morgana's control,' replied Gwen. She turned desperately to Flora. 'I bet she sent them here so even if we get out through the bars, we won't be able to escape!'

'What are we going to do, Gwen? How— ?' Flora broke off with a shriek of terror as a particularly large wolf flung itself at the bars where she had been trying to squeeze out, and there was a loud cracking noise. One of the bars there had begun to break. 'They're destroying the barrier! They're going to get in!'

Don't panic, Gwen told herself, but it was

hard. They were completely trapped in the cave. If the wolves broke through the bars, there would be no escape for them. Her heart thudded wildly.

Flora sank to the ground, burying her head in her knees. Her flute fell from her pocket and rolled on to the cave floor.

Isabella crouched down. 'It's all right. We'll think of something,' she comforted Flora.

Gwen stared at Flora's flute, frowning. Seeing the instrument reminded her of Bethany's dogs. They'd hated the high noise that Gwen and Flora had made when they had been playing their instruments earlier that day. Gwen could see them in her head, yapping and protesting. She picked

 up the flute. It was only the faintest of hopes, but at least it was one. 'Flora!

Play some notes!'

'What?' Flora lifted her tear-stained face.

Gwen thrust the flute into her hands. 'Play something – anything high. The noise,' she explained. 'It might make the wolves go away! Remember Bethany's dogs?'

She saw understanding light up in Flora's eyes. 'You think it might work on the wolves too?'

'We might as well try and see!'

Scrambling to her feet, Flora lifted the flute and very shakily blew a string of high notes.

Instantly the leader of the wolves jerked as if he'd just been shot with an arrow. Throwing back his head, he howled.

'He doesn't like it!' cried Gwen, encouraged. 'Play more. Make the notes as high as you can!'

Flora blew another string of screeching notes. The wolves all started to yelp. Several

of them backed away from the cave. Gwen ran to the rocky bars blocking the cave entrance. Maybe she could help by joining in too. She didn't have her harp, but she could still make some noise. Picking up a stone from the floor, she ran it up and down the bars hoping it would produce a high-pitched sound, but it just made a clunking noise. She threw the stone down. What she needed was something really hard, something like a diamond.

A diamond!

Gwen whirled round. 'Isabella! Please could I borrow your necklace?'

Isabella didn't stop to ask why. She pulled it over her head and threw it to Gwen. Holding it so the diamond was  in contact with the ridges on the bars of crystal and rock, Gwen ran the diamond up and down. There was a high-pitched squealing noise like chalk pressing on a slate. It added to the notes Flora was playing. The wolves fell back from the bars of the caves and retreated hastily to the trees, their savage howls changing to protesting barks.

'We did it!' gasped Flora, pausing for a second before starting to play again.

'Oh, well done, girls!' said Isabella. 'And look! The wolves have broken the crystal bars – there's a space big enough for you to get through!'

'We can escape!' exclaimed Flora.

Isabella grabbed her hand in excitement, but

Gwen had realised something. Her shoulders slumped. 'Wait a moment,' she said heavily. 'We might have made the wolves retreat, but they're still out there waiting for us.' She pointed towards them with one hand while still running the diamond along the bars with the other. 'Can you see them out there between the trees? If we get out of the cave, they'll just attack us.'

Isabella and Flora stared at her.

'There must be something we can do,' said Flora in dismay.

Gwen swallowed. 'I don't think there is.' For once she was all out of ideas. There was no way they could escape.

'Wait a moment!' Isabella said suddenly. 'I might be able to help. Keep making noise,' she urged the girls. 'My plan will work best if the wolves are clustered together in the trees.'

Gwen began to run the diamond pendant up and down more quickly, and Flora struck up again with her high-pitched flute playing. 'What are you going to do, Isabella?' Gwen asked.

'Now that I am free, I have my powers back. I think I can use them to help us.' Isabella looked at the wolves. 'Let me see,' she murmured to herself. 'Hornets. . .? Wasps. . .? Fleas. . .? No, the wolves shouldn't be punished for Morgana using them for her own evil ends. It's not their fault.' A smile suddenly lit up her face. 'Yes, I know what I'll do!' She turned to the girls. 'I'm going to cast a spell. Hopefully it will distract the wolves for a short while, giving us enough time to get out of this cave and escape without them seeing us. How fast can you run?'

'Um. . .' said Gwen with a glance at Flora.

'Not very,' Flora admitted honestly.

Isabella looked worried. 'Oh dear. We're a long way from the Lake.'

'But we won't have to run all the way there,' Gwen pointed out. 'Once we're in the trees, we can call for Moonlight.'

'Moonlight?' Isabella questioned.

'He's a magic stallion,' explained Gwen. 'He can gallop incredibly fast. He's waiting somewhere out there for us.'

'Perfect,' said Isabella, her eyes shining. 'So all we need to do is get far enough past the wolves so that Moonlight can come to you.'

'But how do we do that?' asked Flora.

Isabella smiled. 'Watch and see!' she said.

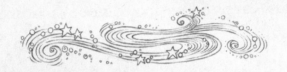

8

Escape!

Isabella went to the entrance of the cave and held up her arms. Gwen shared a bewildered look with Flora. What was Isabella doing?

The sister began to chant a spell:

'Butterfly friends, please come to me,
Confuse, distract, help us break free.'

Gwen frowned. What did the spell mean? What was going to happen?

'Watch,' Isabella said softly, guessing what Gwen was thinking. 'Help is coming!'

As they stared out from the cave, a large blue butterfly swooped down through the trees. Two small cream butterflies danced lightly through the air after it. A fourth with spotted red wings followed, and then a fifth, and suddenly hundreds of beautiful butterflies seemed to be flying down into the clearing!

Flora and Gwen gasped. The butterflies' delicate wings fluttered as they surrounded the wolves, flying around their heads in glittering, rainbow-coloured clouds. The wolves snapped and snarled at them, but the butterflies simply flew around their heads and bodies, confusing and distracting them.

'Quick!' said Isabella, squeezing through the space between the broken crystal bars at the cave mouth. 'This is our chance to escape!'

Gwen and Flora followed her eagerly. There were so many butterflies in the air that the wolves couldn't see the cave and didn't notice the girls slipping out between the bars.

'This way!' whispered Isabella, leading the girls away down a nearby track. She broke into a run. Gwen and Flora held hands and raced after her, jumping over tree roots and brambles, running until their breath was coming in short gasps and their lungs felt as if they were going to burst.

Isabella finally stopped. 'The first part of our escape is over. Can you call Moonlight now? Will he come?'

'Where are we? Do you remember where

we left him, Gwen? We might be too far away,' panted Flora.

'But maybe that doesn't matter,' Gwen put in. 'Remember how he came to the garden today when we needed him?' She didn't know if it would work, but shutting her eyes, she gripped her pendant and pictured the white stallion. *Moonlight! Help us! Please come! We need you, boy!* she thought desperately.

They waited, but for a moment nothing happened. 'It's not working. He's not coming!' said Flora, pacing up and down anxiously and looking back behind them to make sure the wolves weren't approaching. But suddenly there was a whinny, and then Moonlight came galloping into the clearing.

'Moonlight!' cried Gwen in delight. The stallion stopped and pushed his nose against her chest.

'I knew you'd come,' Gwen told him. 'Thank you!' Taking hold of his mane, she swung herself on to his warm back.

'Quickly, girls!' Isabella urged. 'My butterfly friends can only keep the wolves distracted for a short while longer.'

Flora scrambled up behind Gwen. 'I'm ready.'

'Then gallop to the Lake with all the speed you can!' Isabella urged. 'I shall see you both there.' Clapping her hands, she disappeared in a flash of silvery light.

Gwen heard the sound of the wolves' howls coming towards them through the trees. With every second, the menacing creatures were getting closer. She touched Moonlight's sides with her heels. 'To the Lake, Moonlight!'

The horse didn't need telling twice. He

plunged away through the trees at an incredible speed! Gwen had never ridden so fast in her life. The tree trunks whizzed by, the wind whipping tears from the corners of her eyes. She clasped Moonlight's mane as tightly as she could and let the world blur around her.

It felt like they had only been galloping a few minutes when the stallion came to a stop. Gwen and Flora looked around. They were back beside the glittering Lake. 'That was really fast!' said

Flora, slowly releasing her grip around Gwen's waist.

Nineve was standing at the edge of the Lake, talking to Isabella. Slipping off Moonlight's back, Gwen and Flora ran over.

'Welcome back. You have done incredibly well,' said Nineve, smiling warmly at them.

'Isabella has been telling me how you freed her and escaped from the cave despite Morgana's evil plans to trap you there.'

'Thank you, girls,' Isabella said gratefully. 'I mean that from the bottom of my heart.' She looked towards the purple mist swirling over the centre of the Lake. 'Now I want nothing more than to see my home and my sisters again.'

'Two of your sisters already await you on the island,' said Nineve.

'And we'll free the others,' Gwen promised. 'No matter what Morgana does to try and stop us.'

Flora nodded. 'We're not going to let her have Avalon. It's yours and you all belong there. We're going to help you restore its magic again.'

Isabella smiled at them again gratefully. 'Thank you.'

'Come to the island now,' Nineve told the girls. She waved her hands and a silver cloud swirled around their feet. Before they knew it, they found themselves being lifted into the air. They floated up and came to rest on the water's surface. The purple mist in the centre of the lake parted, revealing a path that led to Avalon. Gwen and Flora followed Nineve and Isabella across the water towards the island.

Avalon was just as Gwen had remembered it from the last time she'd been there. There was a stone house up a short path with smoke coming from the chimney and light spilling from the windows. As Gwen glanced around, she saw a muddy puddle where there should have been a lovely pond. Only a few green lily pads floated on the shallow water. However, one thing *was* different, she realised. Last time they had been there, the air on the island had been very still, silence seeming to hang over everything, but now a few insects were darting and swooping around. Small bright butterflies were fluttering between the branches of the apple trees and bumblebees were buzzing contentedly.  The place might look quite barren still, but it felt somehow more alive with the insects returning.

When we get all the Spell Sisters back, Avalon's magic will return, Gwen thought. Feeling a fierce rush of determination, she lifted her chin. They would do it – they had to! They weren't going to let Morgana win!

'Sisters!' Isabella cried, running up the path to the house. 'Sisters! Are you here?'

The front door opened and Sophia and Lily came out. They cried out in delight when they saw Isabella, and the next second they were running down the path to meet her.

Leaving Nineve to remain guarding the Lake, Gwen and Flora hurried to join the three sisters.

'You rescued Isabella for us!' Sophia said to them, her eyes shining.

'Thank you so much!' said Lily.

'They were so brave,' Isabella told her sisters. 'We've had the most incredible adventure. I will tell you all about it later.' She turned to Gwen and Flora. 'I cannot tell you how happy I am to be home, girls. I want to give you a gift to show my gratitude.'

Gwen's hand instinctively reached for her necklace. Alongside the blue pendant were two small gemstones – a fire agate and an emerald – that Sophia and Lily had given to her after she and Flora had helped each of them return to Avalon.

Isabella's brown eyes fell on the stones and she smiled. 'I see my sisters have already had the same thought. I too shall add to your necklace. I hope the gem I give you will be of use one day in your fight against Morgana.'

She stepped forward and held her hands out, palms upward. She murmured a word that Gwen couldn't catch and a large butterfly with golden-brown wings edged with blue came swooping down through the air. It landed in Isabella's palms, its wings beating for a moment before becoming still.

Isabella offered her hands to the girls. Gwen caught her breath as she realised that the butterfly was holding a glowing jewel between its front two legs.

'Amber,' said Isabella. 'Take it and place it next to my sisters' gems.'

Gwen reached out and took the gem from the butterfly. It was smooth and shining, its surface swirling with different shades of gold and orange. She touched it to the necklace and jumped as there was a golden flash. She took her hands away and looked down to see that Isabella's gem had magically attached itself next to the emerald.

'I hope it shall prove useful when you need it most,' Isabella said with a smile. She gently lifted the butterfly into the air and it swooped away. Lily and Sophia joined her and all the sisters linked arms.

'We'd better go,' said Gwen, seeing that the sun was starting to set.

'We hope we'll see you both again very soon,' said Sophia.

'We'll be back when we've rescued another of your sisters,' Flora promised.

'May the magic of Avalon watch over you both!' the sisters called as Flora and Gwen turned and ran back down the path to where Nineve was waiting.

'Well done,' the Lady of the Lake said. 'Thank you for helping today. I do hope you won't get into trouble for coming here.'

Flora looked worried. 'Mother's bound to have come looking for us in the rose garden. She'll be wondering where we are.'

'Well, even if she is and we get into trouble, at least we rescued Isabella,' Gwen pointed out.

Flora nodded, but she still looked anxious.

'Let us return to Moonlight,' said Nineve.

They followed her back across the Lake. Moonlight lifted his head as the girls stepped from the water on to the rocks. Nineve squeezed their hands. 'Go with all speed. I will use my magic to try and find the next Spell Sister and contact you as soon as I find anything out.'

'I wonder where she will be,' said Gwen.

'And what Morgana will try to do to stop

us,' added Flora.

Nineve's eyes regarded them warmly. 'Whatever she tries, I am sure the two of you will be up to the challenge. The pendant chose well when it picked you.' She smiled and slowly backed away. 'Farewell!' she cried and with that, she sank down into the Lake.

'She's gone,' Gwen said softly.

'And it's time we left too,' said Flora. 'Come on, let's go!'

Back at the Manor

Sitting once more on Moonlight's back, the girls raced away through the forest. 'I'm so glad we were able to rescue Isabella,' Gwen said over her shoulder to Flora.

'I am too. I just hope we're not going to get into too much trouble,' replied Flora.

'Perhaps everyone will have been so busy getting ready for the party tonight that they won't have noticed we've gone,' said Gwen hopefully.

'Even if they haven't noticed we've been missing, look at the state of us!' said Flora. 'We're covered in mud, and you've torn your dress. Mother will be furious when she sees.'

'Then let's just hope she doesn't see,' said Gwen. 'Maybe we can sneak in without being noticed.'

She realised they were approaching the wall surrounding the manor house.

'Whoa, boy.' Gwen pulled the stallion's mane to try and slow him down. She and Flora had got away with him jumping into the garden earlier that afternoon, but she didn't want to risk it twice. If anyone saw them on the white horse, it would take a huge amount of explaining. 'It might be better if you leave us by the gates this time,' she told him.

Moonlight obediently slowed to a trot and then a walk. He halted by the gates and Gwen and Flora slipped off his back. Gwen stroked him. 'Thank you, Moonlight. You've been wonderful today. We'd never have got to the Lake, or rescued Isabella, or got back in time for the party without you. Thank you for coming when we needed you.'

Moonlight nuzzled her.

Flora stroked his nose. 'I think I even enjoyed my first jump.' She looked round and pulled a face. 'But what I'm not going to enjoy is trying to get back into the house with no one seeing us!'

Moonlight tossed his mane and then swung round and galloped away, back across the meadows towards the forest.

Gwen peered round the gates. There was no

one in the garden. 'Come on! Let's go to the rose garden first and pick up my harp.'

She and Flora raced across the lawn. To their relief the harp was still beside the bench. Gwen tucked it under her travelling cloak and then they ran to the side of the house, where there was a small wooden door. Gwen turned the handle. The door opened on to a narrow servants' staircase. 'Let's go up to our chamber this way!' she said.

'Hold on! Take your cloak off first in case anyone sees us and wonders why we've still got our outdoors clothes on,' said Flora.

They shrugged off their cloaks and, bundling them into their arms, they hurried up the stairs and then crossed the landing towards their bedchamber. They had just reached the door when they heard Bethany's voice behind them. 'Guinevere? Flora?'

They both froze. Gwen clutched her cloak in front of her, hiding the harp underneath it. She looked over her shoulder. Bethany had just come out of her chamber. She was wearing a beautiful red velvet dress with matching ribbons in her hair.

'Aunt Matilda's been looking for you. She was wondering where you had got to,' Bethany said. Gwen was suddenly very thankful that the light in the corridor was dim now it was evening and that the back of their robes were less muddy than the front.

'Why aren't you changed yet?' Bethany asked, looking at their everyday dresses. 'My party is about to start.'

'We were just going to,' Gwen said quickly, hoping Bethany wouldn't come any closer and see the mud on their faces. They would be in so much trouble if anyone realised the mess they were in.

'We'll be ready in a minute,' stammered Flora.

'You will need to be or you will be late,' said Bethany. She sighed and looked sorrowfully at Flora. 'Really, Flora. Surely you know how important it is for young ladies to be punctual on all occasions. I would have expected lateness from Guinevere, but not from you. I had been going to ask you if you would like to sit by me at the table and read my book of poems, but now I think perhaps I should ask someone else.'

She tutted, sounding very like Aunt Matilda for a moment, and then swept away down the stairs.

Gwen glanced at Flora, sure she'd be upset. 'Are you all right?'

But to her surprise, Flora was not looking unhappy but cross. 'That was a horrible thing to say about you!' she said hotly. 'I wouldn't want to sit with her anyway after that!' She went into the bedchamber and Gwen followed. 'I don't want to read her poems!' Flora declared.

Gwen grinned. 'I wonder what Bethany would say if she knew what we'd been doing today?'

'I know!' Flora put her hands to her chest and cried dramatically. 'Ah, me!'

They both giggled. 'She'd have probably fainted if she'd seen the wolves,' said Gwen.

'Maybe I don't want to be like her after all,' said Flora with feeling.

'Good! I can't imagine cousin Bethany *ever* having an adventure,' said Gwen. 'Come on! Let's get changed. We can clean these clothes in the morning.'

They got out of their dirty clothes and put on their new dresses. Then they tidied up each other's hair and washed their faces using a jug and a bowl of water standing on a low table.

'How do I look?' Flora said, checking her reflection in the looking glass.

'Exactly like a young lady who's about to play at her cousin's birthday celebration should,'

said Gwen. 'What about me?'

'Very neat and tidy – for once!' said Flora. She took her flute out of the pocket of her old clothes. 'So, are you ready to entertain everyone?'

Gwen nodded. 'I am.' She picked up her harp and stroked it fondly. 'You know, I'm never going to complain about having to practise playing my harp again. Being able to play music proved very useful today.'

Flora chuckled. 'I hope, when we go downstairs we make a better noise then we did in the cave, though!'

'Do you know what I hope?' Gwen said.

'Let me see,' said Flora, pretending to think. 'Hmm. Could it be that we have another adventure again very soon?'

Gwen nodded. 'Oh, yes!'

Flora grinned. 'Me too!'

'Flora! Guinevere!' Aunt Matilda's voice called up the stairs.

The two girls smiled at each other and ran out to join the party.

In a Forest Clearing

Morgana Le Fay stormed out of her lair in the massive hollow tree. She moved so quickly that her raven flew up from her shoulder with a surprised squawk.

Morgana barely noticed. Her face was deathly pale, her jet eyes burning with fury. 'I cannot believe I have failed again!' she muttered, stalking into the dark trees. Overhead, the stars were just starting to shine in the dusky sky. 'Another Spell Sister of Avalon is free, and another of my sister's powers is lost to me!'

A swarm of flies swooped down and buzzed in front of her face. Morgana gave an enraged shriek and swiped at them with her hands. 'Those girls are the bane of my life,' she snarled. 'But they will not thwart my plans again!' A calculating look came into her eyes. 'The other powers I have taken from my sisters remain, and the next time the mortal girls try and interfere, I shall be ready and waiting. Nothing shall prevent me from taking Avalon as mine. Nothing!' She threw back her head and laughed.

The raven flew down to her shoulder again,

and the night darkened to a velvet-black around them. . .

BAKE YOUR OWN DELICIOUS BUTTERFLY CUPCAKES!

Butterflies are wonderful, beautiful insects, and without their help Gwen, Flora and Isabella might never have escaped from the cave. Try this special recipe for butterfly cupcakes and see if you can make your cakes look as pretty as the real thing!

Ingredients:

+ 100g caster sugar
+ 100g butter, softened
+ 2 large eggs
+ 100g self-raising flour
+ ½ tsp baking powder
+ ½ tsp Vanilla essence
+ 15ml (1 tablespoon) milk
+ Buttercream icing

Be very careful when using an oven – always ask a grown-up to help you!

TOP TIP

+ *Try adding special finishing touches to your cupcakes, like sprinkling with icing sugar or hundreds and thousands. You could even add some food colouring to your buttercream icing to really make them stand out!*

METHOD

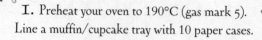

1. Preheat your oven to 190°C (gas mark 5). Line a muffin/cupcake tray with 10 paper cases.

2. Place the sugar, butter, eggs, flour, baking powder, vanilla essence and milk in a large bowl and mix until pale and creamy.

3. Use a spoon and divide your mixture evenly between your papercases – the cupcakes will rise slightly, so only fill the cases halfway to the top.

4. Place the tray in the oven for 15-20 minutes until the cupcakes are risen, golden and firm to the touch. Then transfer the cupcakes to a cooling rack and leave to cool. *Remember to ask a grown-up when you use the oven.*

5. When the cakes are cool, slice the tops off and create a small indent in each cake. Put the sliced tops to one side (you'll need them later!) and fill the holes in the top of the cupcakes with buttercream icing.

6. Take the sliced tops and cut them in half. Arrange two halves on top of each cupcake, nestled in the buttercream, so they look like the wings of a butterfly in flight.

7. Eat, share, enjoy!

VISIT WWW.SPELLSISTERS.CO.UK AND

Plus lots of other enchanted extras!

Spell Sisters news

Explore Avalon

More about Gwen and Flora's quest

Spell Sister profiles

Activity sheets

Wallpapers

Your chance to get in touch with us

ENTER THE MAGICAL WORLD OF AVALON!